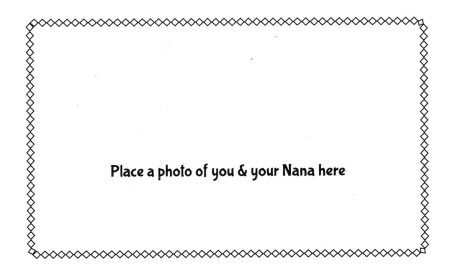

Place a photo of you & your Nana here

For my Nana, Louise Godfrey McNeil, the best Nana ever!— I.S.

Second Edition Published 2014

Paperback ISBN: 978-1-62395-584-7
eISBN: 978-1-62395-585-4

Published in the United States
by Xist Publishing
www.xistpublishing.com

My Nana and Me

written by **Irene Smalls**

illustrated by **Cathy Ann Johnson**

My Nana and Me had a tea party
and all my dolls came
We had tea and cake and ate and ate
bread pudding and apple pie.

I wore Nana's Sunday hat and shoes.

And, I put on a show.
I danced like a
ballerina and sang.

My Nana
clapped and
clapped and
clapped.

Then we played hide–and–seek.
My Nana can never find me.

I am the smartest girl in the world.
I know because my Nana told me so
and she knows everything.

My Nana's a giant – she's so tall!
She can reach and touch the sky.
She has a big, long skirt that
I hide behind sometimes.

Then Nana calls me her baby girl,
but I'm not a baby, I'm BIG!

My Nana gets down on
her knees to talk to me

We rub noses
the way Eskimos kiss.

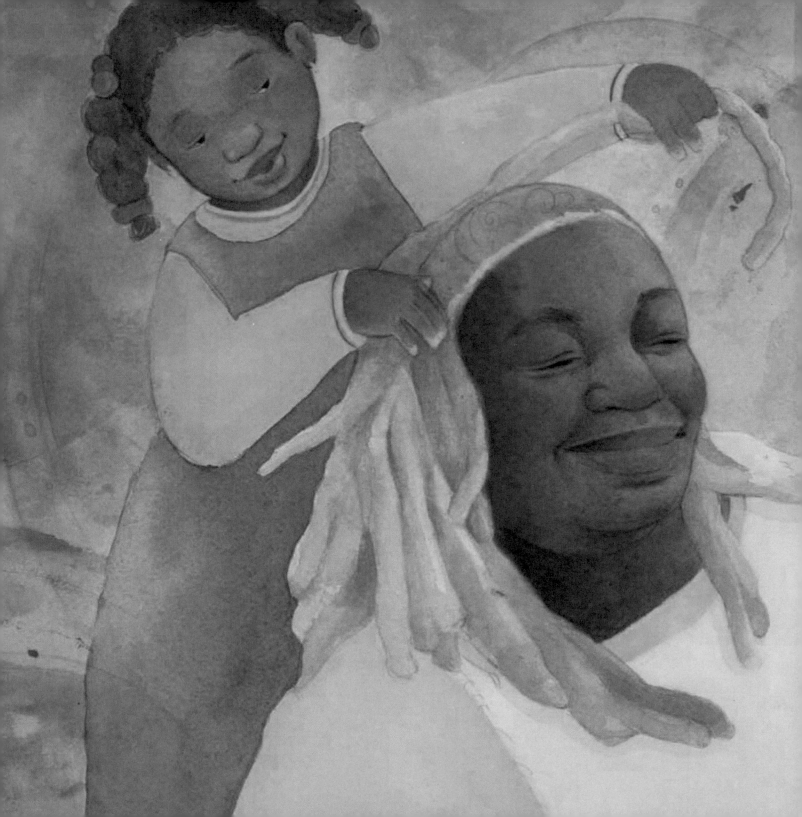

I comb and plait my Nana's hair
overbraid and underbraid,
overbraid and underbraid.

Next we play pat-a-cake till half past eight.

That's when I take a bath.
My Nana washes me with hands that tickle my nose and dance on my back as she sings,

"Onchi monchi bunchi bunch, onchi monchi bunchi bunch"

She calls me her
sweetening girl
and laughs and
laughs and laughs.
She sits me on her knee
and reads to me
story after story
after story.

When I ask Nana why,
am I her sweetening girl?
Nana says,
"because there's a sky,
because there's a sea."
But mostly
because there is me!

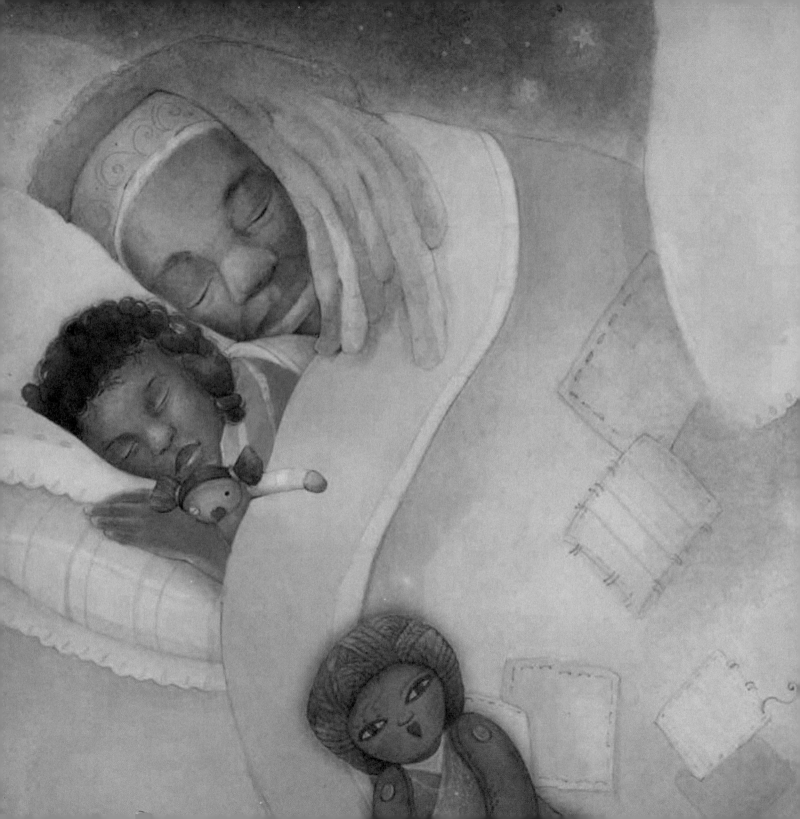

Then, Nana
such a sleepyhead
lies down on my bed,
and then

so do I.